WITCHES

By Cheryl Christian

Illustrated by Wish Williams

Star Bright Books
New York

Published in the United States of America by Star Bright Books, Inc., 30-19 48th Avenue, Long Island City, NY 11101.

The name Star Bright Books and the Star Bright Books logo are registered trademarks of Star Bright Books, Inc. Please visit www.starbrightbooks.com. For bulk orders, email: orders@starbrightbooks.com, or call customer service at: (718) 784-9112.

Paperback ISBN-13: 978-1-59572-283-6

Star Bright Books / NY / 00103110
Printed in China (WKT) 10 9 8 7 6 5 4 3 2 1

Library of Congress Cataloging-in-Publication Data

Christian, Cheryl.
 Witches / by Cheryl Christian ; illustrated by Wish Williams. -- paperback ed.
    p. cm.
 Summary: Illustrations and rhyming text celebrate witches' fun of Halloween.
 ISBN 978-1-59572-283-6
 [1. Witches--Fiction. 2. Halloween--Fiction.] I. Williams, Wish, ill. II. Title.
 PZ8.3.C4566Wit 2011
 [E]--dc22
                                    2010050909

Special thanks to everyone at Star Bright Books for all their help. – C.C.

Witches at their cauldron,
witches at their brew.

Throwing in some spiders' webs,
and a bone or two.

Any kind of
smelly,
slimy,
sticky
stuff will do.

Witches take a spoonful, everyone must taste.

Witches very busy,
everyone in haste.

Witches on their broomsticks, flying through the night.

Witches screeching screeches, what a fearful sight.

Witches in their dark capes, wearing witchy hats.

Witches on their witchy way, followed by their cats.

Witches ringing doorbells, running through the street.

Witches having lots of fun . . .

. . . calling "TRICK OR TREAT!"